21165

Skeleton
Man

Skeleton Man

JOSEPH BRUCHAC

■ HARPERCOLLINS*PUBLISHERS*

Skeleton Man

Copyright © 2001 by Joseph Bruchac

All rights reserved. No part of this book may be used or reproduced in any
manner whatsoever without written permission except in the case of brief
quotations embodied in critical articles and reviews. Printed in the United
States of America. For information address HarperCollins Children's Books, a
division of HarperCollins Publishers, 1350 Avenue of the Americas, New York,
NY 10019.

www.harperchildrens.com

Library of Congress-in-Publication Data

Bruchac, Joseph.

Skeleton man / by Joseph Bruchac.

p. cm.

Summary: After her parents disappear and she is turned over to the care of a
strange "great-uncle," Molly must rely on her dreams about an old Mohawk
story for her safety and maybe even for her life.

ISBN 0-06-029075-7 — ISBN 0-06-029076-5 (lib. bdg.)

[1. Psychopaths—Fiction. 2. Kidnapping—Fiction. 3. Mohawk Indians—
Fiction. 4. Indians of North America—New York (State)—Fiction.] I. Title.

PZ7.B82816 Sk 2001   00-054345

[Fic]—dc21   CIP

                                                                    AC

Typography by Hilary Zarycky

1 2 3 4 5 6 7 8 9 10

❖

First Edition

21165

For my wife, Carol, and my daughter-in-law, Jean, who are two of the bravest people I've ever known, and for all the young women who have yet to discover the courage that lives in their hearts.

ACKNOWLEDGMENTS

I could not have written this book without the many lessons I've been taught by such tradition bearers as the late Alice Shenandoah Papineau/Dewasentah (Onondaga), Grandmother Doris Minkler (Abenaki), and my great friend Gayle Ross (Cherokee). They have helped me understand even more deeply how different the strong women in our traditional American Indian stories are from the dependent damsels of European folktales who hope for a prince to rescue them. Not only do our Native American heroines take care of their own rescues, they often save the men, too!

Contents

Skeleton Man

Footsteps on the Stair

'M NOT SURE how TO begin this story. For one thing, it's still going on. For another, you should never tell a story unless you're sure how it's going to end. At least that's what my sixth-grade teacher, Ms. Shabbas, says. And I'm not sure at all. I'm not sure that I even know the beginning. I'm not sure if I'm a minor character or the heroine. Heck, I'm not even sure I'll be around to tell the end of it. But I don't think anyone else is going to tell this story.

Wait! What was that noise?

I listen for the footsteps on the stairs, footsteps much heavier than those an elderly man should make. But it's quiet, just the usual spooky nighttime creaking of this old house. I don't hear anyone coming now. If I don't survive, maybe they'll all realize I should have been taken seriously and then warn the world!

Warn the world. That's pretty melodramatic, isn't it? But that is one of the things I do well, melodrama. At least that is what Ms. Shabbas says. Her name is Maureen Shabbas. But Ms. Showbiz is what we all call her, because her main motive for living seems to be torturing our class with old Broadway show tunes. She starts every day by singing a few bars of one and then making it the theme for the day. It is so disgustingly awful that we all sort of like it. Imagine someone who loves to imitate Yul Brynner in *The King and I*, a woman with an Afro, no less, getting up and singing "Shall We Dance?" in front of a classroom of appalled adolescents. Ms. Showbiz. And she has the nerve to call *me* melodramatic!

But I guess I am. Maybe this whole thing is a product of my overactive imagination. If that turns out to be so, all I can say is who wouldn't have an overactive imagination if they'd heard the kind of stories I used to hear from Mom and Dad?

within: *tschick-a-tschick-tschick-a-tschick*. Then a dry voice called out to her.

"My niece," Skeleton Man whispered. "Come into the lodge. I have been waiting for you."

That voice made her skin crawl. "Where are my parents?" she asked.

"They are here. They are here inside," Skeleton Man whispered. "Come in and be with them."

"No," the girl said, "I will not come inside."

"Ah," Skeleton Man replied in his dry, thin voice, "that is all right. I will come out for you."

Then Lazy Uncle, the Skeleton Man, walked out of the lodge. His dry bones rubbed together as he walked toward the little girl: *tschick-a-tschick-tschick-a-tschick*.

The girl began to run, not sure where to go. Skeleton Man would have caught her and eaten her if it hadn't been for that rabbit she'd rescued from the river. It appeared on the path before her.

"I will help you because you saved me," said the rabbit. "Follow me."

Then the rabbit helped the little girl outwit Skeleton Man. It even showed her how to bring everyone Skeleton Man had eaten back to life.

My mom and dad told me stories like that all the time. Before they vanished. Disappeared. Gone, just like that.

I was on TV when they disappeared. You probably saw me on *Unsolved Mysteries*. The news reporter said into her microphone, "Child left alone in house for over three days, terrified, existing on cornflakes and canned food." Actually I went to school on Tuesday and called out for pizza once. Mom had left money on her dresser when they went out that Saturday evening and never returned.

I didn't know they hadn't come back until Sunday. I had gone to bed Saturday evening, expecting them to wake me up when they came home, like they always did. But not this time. When I woke up that Sunday morning, I knew something was totally wrong. The house was quiet. Usually my parents were both up way before me. I should have heard Dad in the kitchen, banging the pans around. Sunday was always his day for making breakfast and he made a big thing about it. He'd thaw out a whole quart of blueberries from the freezer and warm up some real maple syrup. But no noise came from the kitchen, no pans rattling, no seventies music playing on the kitchen CD player—my dad is a freak for the Eagles and says it is impossible for him to cook without them.

I sat up in bed and held my breath. No rhythmic pounding of my mother running in place in their bedroom down the hall. I looked at the clock—eight thirty. By now Mom should have been halfway through her first set of aerobics, but there were no sounds of thudding sneakers. The only thumping I could hear was my own heart.

Maybe they'd been out so late that they were still sleeping. It had to have been late when they came back because I'd finally drifted off to sleep after midnight, waiting for them.

I stood up and went out into the hall. "Mom? Dad?" No answer.

It seemed to take me forever to reach the door to their room. It was like I was walking underwater. The door was only half shut. I pushed it open, not sure what I'd see. Maybe they'd jump out at me and tickle me and laugh at their joke.

But no one was there. Their bed hadn't been slept in. No one was behind the door or in the closet or anywhere. Not there in the bedroom, not anywhere in the house. And the car was gone from the garage. There was no sign of anyone. It was a cold gray day, as gray as the long driveway leading down to the road. I didn't go outside to look around. I could tell it was going to rain soon. I didn't go to a neighbor's house because I couldn't. We live out in the country without any neighbors anywhere near us.

It was freaky, that's for sure, but I wasn't scared. Not yet. I just felt it in my bones that they'd be back. I went into the living room and turned on the TV, waiting. I have no idea what I watched, even though I sat there for hours. I don't know if it was sports or cartoons or the home-shopping network. For some reason I never turned on the news, even though it might have had something on if they'd been in an accident. But that couldn't be it. Someone would have come to the house to tell me, or there would have been a phone call. I looked at the phone, hoping it would ring and praying it wouldn't.

Rain began to hammer at the windows at about noon, and I went around the house making sure they were all shut. I looked out my bedroom window at Dad's toolshed. Its one window was shut, and I was glad about that. I didn't want to go outside in that cold rain.

Finally, at about two in the afternoon, I decided I'd make breakfast. I set the table for the three of us, got out the juice and syrup and blueberries and milk and everything, even napkins that I folded so they stood up on the plates. They'd come in, all apologetic, and I would say, "No problem. Look, I even fixed breakfast for us." I can't explain why I thought anyone would want breakfast in mid-afternoon. It made sense then. I must have been preoccupied, what with listening for their car to pull in, because I made the pancakes all wrong so that they were runny and then I burned them.

I laughed some when I was cleaning up the mess I'd made, just knowing they'd come in right in the middle of it and tease me and tell me it was all right, and then we'd all go out for dinner. But it didn't happen that way. Finally, at about 8 P.M. I ended up eating cornflakes with warm milk and what was left of the thawed, soggy blueberries. I got my pillow and some blankets and made a bed for myself on the couch in front of the TV. That way they'd see me there when they came in. They'd be sorry and I'd be upset, but I would finally forgive them. I also didn't feel like going upstairs all by myself. Besides, Dad would pick me up and carry me to my room like he used to when I was a little girl. I knew I was much too big for that now, but the thought of it—of my dad's strong arms lifting me, my mom patting my face with her hand—calmed me down, and I went off to sleep.

When I woke up the next morning, on Monday, and found out I was still alone in the house, I guess I should have called someone. But I didn't. I didn't get dressed for school. I didn't even turn off the TV, which had been going all night. I just sat and looked at the phone. The first time it rang, I jumped a mile. It was from work for Mom. I told them she was sick. I did the same thing when Dad's partner, Al Mondini, called from the bank to see where he was. Mom and I always call him Almond Al.

"Shouldn't you be at school, Molly?" Almond Al said.

"I should, but I'm sick, too," I said. I could hear the long pause at the other end of the line. If I was sick, he was wondering, how come I was talking on the phone now. So, just like my parents always said, one lie had to lead to another. "I'm better than they are, though," I said in a quick, nervous voice. "I mean, I didn't lose my voice like they did and so that is why I am answering the phone. But it hurts to talk, so I have to hang up now. Bye."

Maybe Almond Al was the one who got suspicious and called the police.

That night I went around to all the doors to make sure they were still locked, and I checked the windows. I turned off the TV and then, because it seemed too quiet, I turned it on again. Not real loud, just on. I went upstairs and turned on the radio in Mom and Dad's bedroom, and I lay there for a while on top of their bed, listening to classical music. I still wasn't scared, but after a while I got up and went into my bedroom. I locked my door and put a chair in front of it. There's this song that Mom taught me once, one that she called a Lonesome Song, a song you sing when you're all alone and need a friend. If a friend hears you, they'll sing back to you.

I sang that Lonesome Song very softly to myself.

"Hey yoo, hey yah neh . . ."

I kept on singing it. Even though no one answered, it made me feel less alone and I fell asleep.

The next morning was easier. I got up, got dressed, had more cornflakes, brushed my teeth, and caught the school bus at the bottom of our driveway. I didn't say anything to anyone about Mom and Dad being gone. They're on a trip, I was telling myself now. Everything is fine. They'll be back. I even remembered to make up a really official-looking note on my computer saying that I'd been sick and that was why I'd missed school, and I signed it with my mom's name. But maybe the way I worded it wasn't quite right. I know the woman in the office looked at me strangely when I handed it to her with a big smile. Maybe she was the one who made the call. Or maybe it was Ms. Shabbas. I smiled and laughed so much in class that day that Ms. Shabbas looked over at me with one eyebrow raised the way she always does when she thinks something is wrong. But I avoided talking with her. If I talked with her about it, then it would mean something was wrong.

I was so sure that everything would work out. I never doubted. Not even when the people came to the house the next night and started questioning me. Nor when the Social Services lady and the two cops escorted me out. I just kept saying, "I have to stay here. They'll be back." I even said that to the news-people when they showed up. I don't know who called them. Maybe they just sensed it the way sharks smell blood and come swarming in when something has been wounded.

It just looks like I was crying on that TV show. The microphones make your voice sound all weird, like you are hysterical or something. And the lights make your eyes look all wild and scared. They even made mine water so much that you might have thought I was crying. I wasn't. I knew Mom and Dad would be back.

I still know they'll be back. But I don't want to talk about that. I just wanted to explain that I was never afraid. Not at all. Until later that night when this old guy showed up.

"Molly," the Social Services woman said, "someone is here for you, one of your relatives."

That was a big surprise to me. I didn't know I had any relatives anywhere near here. Mom is an orphan and all Dad's closest relatives are dead. It's a really sad story, how his brothers died in a car accident and his sister drowned, and then there was this big fire while Dad was away at school and his parents were in the house. That left only his two aunts to raise him, but they were old people and they died before I was born. I think that's the reason why we've never gone up to the reservation. There's nobody close to Dad there anymore, and that makes him too sad. But Dad had said that there were cousins and that maybe sometime we'd get to meet them, although they lived way out in California.

The Social Services woman led me into another room. A tall, elderly, thin man with stooped shoulders, all dressed in gray—even his shoes!—was standing there looking out the window.

"Here's your niece," the Social Services lady said in a chirpy voice. He turned around to look down at me with a face that was so thin it looked like bone. He didn't look Indian. Though his skin was almost as brown as my dad's, it was as if he'd dyed himself that color. His eyes were round and unblinking, like the eyes of an owl. He smiled, and I could see how big his teeth were.

"I don't know him," I said, taking a step backward.

"Of course not," chirped the lady. "He's been out of the country." She smiled at him, and he nodded back at her. They were two adults, and I was just a kid. What could I know about anything? "You see," she said, taking the tone that certain grown-ups use with children and idiots—who are the same in their minds— "this is such a wonderful coincidence. Your great-uncle here moved into our town just two weeks ago without even knowing that your father, his own dear nephew, was here. He just happened to see the story on the news and came right over here. You are his flesh and blood, dear."

I looked up at him again, and he nodded. There was a little smile on his face. It was as if he knew what I was thinking, as if he knew I knew he wasn't who he said he was, but there was nothing I could do to stop this.

"I don't know him," I said again. "I've never heard of him. And I don't care if he *is* my uncle. My parents will be back soon. And my teacher said I could stay with her if you're worried about me being home by myself."

That was true. Ms. Shabbas had left only an hour ago. She had come to the offices where I was being kept. She'd agreed with me that my parents would be back soon, but she had suggested that, just for now, I might like to stay with her, so I wouldn't have to be alone. But Social Services wouldn't hear of it. Not when an actual relative was coming to get me.

The lady shook her head. She was losing her patience. "Dear," she said, "we have checked things very thoroughly."

She turned and gestured to the tall stranger she was determined to hand me over to. The expression on her face said that she was sorry to bother him, but they needed to humor me to keep me from making a scene. He reached into his pocket and pulled out a big wallet. It was covered with snakeskin.

"Here," she said, taking the wallet and holding it out to me.

I put my hands behind my back. I didn't want to touch it.

"Oh!" she said in an exasperated voice. "Look!"

She flipped the wallet open. There was a driver's license with a picture of the man who was saying he was my uncle. The picture looked more human than he did, but it was him. I looked over at him. A horrible thought came to me. Maybe I was the only one who could see him this way. Maybe he looked normal to other people. I snuck a glance at him. He gave me that little nod and knowing smile again. A shiver went down my back.

"Dea-arrr, look *here*," the lady said, her impatient finger pointing to the license. There was his name, the same last name as my family's. She flipped the license over to show me another clear plastic pocket with a photo in it. It was the smiling face of my father, the high-school graduation photo he'd shown me more than once. She flipped again, and there was a picture of my dad and mom's wedding. The photos were just the same as those my dad always carried in his wallet. That wedding photo even seemed to have the same torn corner. . . .

She slapped the wallet shut and handed it back.

"Then it is settled," she said. "Until your parents return, you will be in the custody of your great-uncle."

And that was that. Unlike in a court of law, when grown-ups make a decision about a kid's future there is no appeal.

I was just so worn-out from all the attention that I didn't protest. I let him take me to this old spooky house.

What was that? Footsteps, heavy ones on the stairs.

Now I am afraid.

The Knock on the Door

T'S THE SEVENTH NIGHT that I've been in this house. I should be ready for his routine by now, but I'm not. First there is the all too familiar sound of heavy feet thumping up the stairs: *thump, thump, thump.* Then there is a long silence while he catches his breath. *Thump, thump, thump* and silence. There are exactly thirty-six stairs, so he does this eleven times. The twelfth time is when I hear the wood on the landing creaking. Then comes the worst part. The silence. Because even though he makes noise coming up the stairs, the noise always stops when he reaches the top. Just that first creak when he steps up from the last stair.

And then nothing.

I imagine that his feet don't really move. He just glides half an inch above the rug, like Dracula in the movies. I know that can't be what happens. I know I'm just scaring myself and that it's the thickness of the rug in the hallway that cushions his steps so that I don't hear them. But even so, I find myself getting up from the bed to stand in the middle of the room, staring at the chair I have in front of the door. And I'm thinking, maybe, just maybe, he won't come to my door tonight. Maybe he'll just go down the hall and into his own room and hang by his toes from the rafters or whatever he does. Maybe he'll leave me in peace.

As always, I'm holding my breath. I'm listening like a deer does when it catches the scent of a mountain lion and then the wind changes so that it can't smell it anymore. But the deer knows the lion is out there somewhere. Maybe moving away, maybe getting closer, maybe . . .

WHACK-WHACK!

The crack of his bony knuckles against the thick wood of the door makes me jump a mile. But I don't scream, like I did the first night he did this after I was brought here.

"You all right?" he says. His voice isn't all that scary, even though it's muffled by the door and sounds as distant as the voice of a memory or a ghost.

I lean back away from the door, trying to make my voice sound as far away from it as possible.

"I'm okay. I'm in bed. I'm going to sleep," I say. Then I wait.

SNICK! That's it. It's the sound of the lock on the outside. Like every other night, he's locked me in. The first night it scared me, but now it makes me breathe a sigh of relief. I count out under my breath. One, two, three, four, five, six. And then I hear it. The sound of his feet going back down the stairs. And unless he comes floating down the halls at midnight, or maybe flying outside to peer in my windows, that's it for the night. I can try to go to sleep now. I'm locked in and, I guess, safe.

And, like the other nights before this, I will try to not think about what it is that I am

locked in against. I'll try not to think about why there are bars on my windows.

I look around the room. There's not much to see. There's the four-poster bed, the bedside stand, and a table by the window, which is covered with thick purple curtains. The walls are bare, though there are square and rectangular-shaped places where the wood isn't quite so dark. I guess there used to be pictures hanging there. There's no closet, just one of those old stand-up wardrobes. It has only six coat hangers in it, but my stuff is still in the suitcase and the cardboard box I brought with me. I'm not planning on staying long, so I don't want to unpack. All the furniture in the room seems to be pretty old, all made of dark wood. The rug on the floor is new and it is cream colored. It doesn't really go with everything else in the room, but at least it means that things aren't so dark in here. I'm grateful for that because the only light is the one on the nightstand and it's got a 40-watt bulb in it. There's also a light in the bathroom, which is attached to the room. I always leave the bathroom door open with the light turned on.

I walk over to the window. Bad idea, a voice is saying to me. But I'm doing it anyway.

Don't look outside. But I can't help myself. I reach for the curtain, feel the heavy fabric in my hand, pull it back.

The whole world explodes in a great burst of light and sound.

3

The Dream

I DON'T SCREAM. It was only thunder and lightning, a rumble that shook the whole building as if it were a dollhouse rocked by a giant's heavy foot thudding down next to it. When there was lightning Mom always said it was the flashbulb of the Creator taking pictures with a giant camera.

Dad always said thunder is the rumbling steps of the Henos, the Thunder Beings, who live in the sky. They're good guys who throw down lightning like spears to destroy monsters.

But this time, at least, their lightning spears seem to have missed. In that moment of absolute brightness outside, my eyes took their own quick picture, one that made me yank the curtains back in place and get into bed with the covers over my head. What had I seen in the flash of lightning? Down there, on the lawn, his face shaded by a wide-brimmed hat, was a man. A tall man, skinny as a skeleton. He was standing at the door of an old shed. It was my uncle.

My mind is going a million miles a minute now. Why was he there? What is he doing? Am I just being paranoid or am I really in some kind of danger? My mind keeps going back to that shed, too. It's a lot older and bigger than the little plywood one Dad has in back of our house. It doesn't have any windows in it like Dad's shed, just one heavy door with a new padlock on it. What was my uncle going to do in that shed in the middle of the night?

I can't find an answer. So I turn it all off by thinking of Ms. Showbiz singing. I think of her singing that song from the musical about Annie, another orphan—assuming I might be one, which I know I really am not. "Tomorrow, tomorrow . . ." And as I put all my thoughts and fears into imagining her singing I fall asleep. And I dream.

It's like some of the dreams I've had before. I know I am dreaming, but I can't wake up. It is what my dad calls an "aware dream." That is a dream where you know you are a dreamer and, if you are alert enough, you'll get some help from your dream. Someone or something will guide you or give you a message. But I am too busy running to look for a guide. Whatever is chasing me is getting closer. I can feel its hot breath on the back of my neck and I know its bony hands are about to grab me.

Then the dream changes. I am in a cave. I live in that cave and I am not alone there. Someone is sitting in the corner of the cave, his face turned away from me. "Hold out your arm, child!" he says in a rough voice. I hold my arm out toward him, and he reaches back to feel it without looking around. His long, dry fingers squeeze my forearm. "Thin as a stick, thin as a stick," he growls. "Go into the forest and check your snares. You must eat more, my niece. Eat and grow fat."

In an eyeblink I'm not in the cave but in the forest. I'm dressed in deerskin, checking the snares I've placed on the trails. I'm worried

because I haven't caught anything. My uncle will be angry.

Then I see motion in the brush. Something is struggling at the side of the path. It's a rabbit, its hind foot caught in one of my snares. I lift my stick to hit it. But the rabbit looks up at me and speaks.

"Little Sister," the rabbit says, "spare my life, and I will help you save your own life."

I put down my stick and loosen the cord from the rabbit's foot. It doesn't run away when it is free. Instead it looks me in the eye and speaks again.

"Little Sister," the rabbit says, "thank you for sparing me. Now I will tell you what you must know. The one you think is your uncle is not human."

4

Dark Cedars

I CAN STILL hear the rabbit's voice when I open my eyes. I look at the clock next to my bed. It is morning, time to get ready for school. I rummage through my suitcase and the cardboard box and find what I need. I don't feel like putting my clothes into the creepy wardrobe. When I was little my mom read me that book about the wardrobe and the lion and the witch. I wished then that I had a magic wardrobe that I could crawl into and end up in some strange land. Now that I really am in a strange land all I want to do is crawl back home. But if there was some kind of magic door in that wardrobe, it'd probably take me someplace even worse than this.

I take my toothbrush and go into the bathroom. The only good thing about the room is that it has a bathroom connected to it. It means I don't have to go out into the hall or downstairs yet and see him. There's a bathroom built in because the former owners tried to run a bed and breakfast. There's actually an old sign leaning on its side against the house: DARK CEDARS BED AND BREAKFAST. The name alone is enough to scare people away from it. But I think it probably just didn't work out because this place is too far from the center of town, even though it is near Three Falls Gorge, which is the town's main place of "scenic beauty," as our chamber of commerce puts it. When my uncle got this place he took down the sign.

While I am in the bathroom I look at myself in the small, smoky mirror hanging over the sink. I think I have the kind of face that only a mother could love, but both my parents tell me I'm wrong. They think thick eyebrows that almost meet in the middle and ink-black hair that grows so thick I need hedge clippers to trim it are positive assets. "There's so much you can do with that hair," my mother says. Like get it cut short and dyed blond. My nose is okay, not bumpy or too short or too long, but my lips are too thick. My cheeks look as if I have apples stuffed in them, and when I smile my teeth are straight, but there is this gap between my incisors on top. "Braces will do wonders for you, dear." As if, I think. I can't wait until I'm old enough to get a real makeover like they have sometimes on the shopping channel.

Still, though I'm not thrilled with how I look, I don't hate my looks. I can just see lots of room for improvement. And I know that people must like my face at least a little because whenever I smile at someone they almost always smile back. Except for my uncle. I tried smiling at him yesterday. He just studied my face like a scientist looking at some strange new bug until my smile crawled away and died. I won't try that again.

I sigh and lift up my chin. At least I don't look like a terrified victim in some slasher movie. I just look like a kid about to catch the bus. I leave the bathroom and try the door. It's not locked from the outside anymore. It never is by this time. I peek outside carefully, my backpack with a large, empty plastic container in it over my shoulder. No sign of anyone up or down the hall.

As soon as I start down the creaky stairs, he hears me.

"Come down to breakfast," he whispers up the stairs. He's standing at the bottom, half hidden by the old coatrack. He turns and walks away. He doesn't like me to see his face in the morning. Or ever, for that matter.

I go into the sunroom. It looks like it used to be a screened porch once. It has a floor of cold stone tiles and is connected to the back of the house. Its four big windows and sliding glass door were probably meant to let in the sun and give you a view of the garden. But there is no sun today, and there hasn't been a garden out there for a while. The places where flowers once grew are overgrown with nettles and burdock and a few small sumac trees, their leaves all red now that there's been a frost.

Although there's room in the sunroom for several tables, there's just the one. It's a glass-topped table with rusty blue metal legs. The two chairs are made of that same rusty blue metal with curlicue designs. The table is set for one. As always, he's already eaten. At least that's what he says. I've never seen evidence of his breakfast. I see his back as he goes out the sun-room door. I'm never allowed to go out that way toward the big shed in the backyard with heavy-duty hinges on the thick, bolted doors. His toolroom, he says. I wonder again what he was doing out there last night.

"Eat your breakfast," he calls back without turning his head. "You're looking thin."

Then he's gone, and I take my first real breath of the day. The food on the table looks good. I'm hungry. Grapefruit, cereal, toast with butter and jam. I put my backpack under the table between my knees. I take the lid off the plastic container in the backpack and pretend to eat. But each spoonful of cereal, each slice of toast, each piece of fruit goes into the plastic box. I snap the lid onto it and close the back-pack. Then I pretend to wipe my lips with the paper napkin, ball it up, and put it on the now-empty plate.

I'm just in time because, just as he's done every other day, he sticks his head out of the door of the shed to see if I've eaten my food.

"Done," I call out in a cheery voice. Then I stand up and walk to the front door, trying to be as calm as possible, hoping that it will not be locked. It isn't, and I escape down the walk to the corner where the school bus will arrive within five minutes. Time enough to dump the food down the storm drain at the curb edge. Let the rats deal with it.

Super paranoid, that is what you are saying now. Melodramatic. But I'm determined not to eat the food he gives me. I think he puts something into it. When I first got here I ate what he put in front of me automatically. I started having a headache and my heart was racing, and I felt like some kind of zombie. When I went to bed that night I just conked out. I didn't even dream. The next day I started my Tupperware routine. If I'd kept eating that food I'd probably be walking with my arms held out in front of me saying, "Yes, Master!" in a hollow voice whenever he spoke to me.

When the bus comes I take the first seat. Other kids are sitting with friends, but I stay by myself. This isn't the bus I used to take. No one in my class is on it, and people are still checking me out. I haven't been in a hurry to be all bright and cheery with my new busmates, either.

When the bus stops in front of the school,

though, I have to start smiling. This is my place of refuge. I'm safe here. Other kids might groan when they walk through the big front doors, but I breathe a sigh of relief. It's all so routine and boring here. I love it. Although when Laura Loh, who is my second-best friend, waves to me from her locker, I pretend not to see her and just go straight into class. I know she wants to talk to me about Greg Iverson and how cute he is and do I think he likes her . . . and I can't bear it. For some reason I just can't think of anything to say to other kids right now, and all the stuff that used to interest me seems kind of unreal.

In our class it is Don Quixote Day. At least it is for Ms. Showbiz. We are all groaning by the time she finishes belting out her medley from *Man of La Mancha*. I'm groaning the loudest of all because it just makes me feel so safe, so . . . normal. I feel so great that when Ms. Shabbas tells us to open our workbooks, I burst out in laughter that is so loud and inappropriate that everyone, including Ms. Shabbas, looks at me. Maureen Viola, who is my best friend and who sits two seats away, looks at me and mouths the words: "What is wrong with you?"

All of a sudden I feel as if I am about to

burst into tears. I have to put my head down on my desk. What *is* wrong with me? I'm not being tortured or anything. My uncle was kind enough to take me in. He's just a little strange. Maybe I'm the truly strange one with my worries about being drugged and my blockading my door at night and imagining what might be happening in that shed. Too much imagination, that's me.

Ms. Shabbas has a little talk with me that afternoon. She asks me to wait behind when the rest of the class is leaving for gym. She's worried about my behavior. "Is everything all right," she pauses, ". . . at home?"

What home? That is what I want to say. I want to scream and cry and have her hold me in her arms while I sob against her shoulder. But what good would that do? So I give her my patented sunny smile.

"Everything is fine," I say. "Really fine."

But Ms. Shabbas doesn't smile back. "Really?" she says in a soft voice. Then she looks beyond that smile, right into my eyes as if she can see my thoughts. It's not the way my uncle does it, not like someone stealing a part of me. It's not even like an adult looking at a kid who's being unreasonable. It's the way a true friend looks at you when they say they want to help you and really mean it.

"No," I whisper. "It's not."

And then I tell her. I don't tell her everything because now that I'm in school, my fears seem a little foolish, and I don't want her to think I'm being melodramatic. But I tell her how I feel, how weird it is in my uncle's house, how I really, really don't want to be there. She doesn't interrupt or ask questions. She just listens, nodding every now and then. When I'm done I feel lighter, as if I'm no longer carrying a ten-ton truck on my shoulders.

Ms. Shabbas lightly places her hands on my shoulders. She doesn't say I'm being foolish or that I should grow up.

"Sweetheart," she says. "Thank you for telling me." She turns slightly to write something on a card that she hands to me. "Here's my home phone and my cell phone. Call me anytime. Okay? We'll keep an eye on this together, right?"

"Right," I say. And for the rest of the day in school things almost do seem right.

But then I take one more deep breath and the school day is over. That's bad. The only good thing is that it is Wednesday. That means I get to come back to school tomorrow and the next day before the weekend comes, which most kids love because it means we won't have to go back to school for two days. Two whole days.

I walk home because it takes longer than the bus. I stop at a fast-food place to eat enough to kill my appetite. I don't have much money left, and I don't know what I'll do when it runs out. But I try not to worry about that now. There are other, more pressing concerns.

Finally it is getting dark. I can't avoid it anymore. I'm headed back to the house of doom.

Eat and Grow Fat

OU MAY be asking yourself what life is like for me inside that house. Are there spiderwebs everywhere? Bats and centipedes and mold on the walls? Are there chains clanking down in the cellar and ghostly moans coming from the attic?

No. Actually, aside from being dark and set back from the road, it isn't really all that spooky a place to look at. It's a hundred years old, but there are older places in town. And the house is full of modern appliances in the kitchen and the living room. Dishwasher, microwave, a television with a cable hookup. My uncle even has a personal computer. I saw it through the open door of his study once. He spends a lot of his time in that room and I imagine he must be surfing the Net, visiting all the weirdest websites, probably.

What makes that house strange is the way it feels when you get inside it. I saw an old movie once where someone walks into a room and then the door disappears and the walls start moving in. It is something like that. And I always feel as if someone or something is looking at me, but when I turn around there's nothing there.

Then there's the way my uncle acts. Like when you'd expect him to be waiting for me, his niece, to come home, and to ask me how my day went, he's not. He's not here. There's just a note on the front door, not handwritten, but out of his laser printer. "Back later," it reads. "Dinner in fridge."

He's left food for me in the refrigerator for the last two nights as well. The food I'm supposed to eat is on a plate on the top shelf, ready to pop into the microwave. Anyhow, it makes it easier for me. I flip on the garbage disposal and spoon the loathsome stuff, a huge plate of spaghetti with meatballs, down the sink drain.

If I ate everything he gave me—even if it wasn't full of drugs—I'd get as fat as a butterball turkey.

I could go into the living room and watch TV. Or one of the videos from the library of movies he has next to the VCR. There's a lot of stuff that some people think kids like to watch. Mostly Disney movies and cartoons. But I don't want to. It's the thought of having him walk in while I'm watching something. Or, even worse, of him watching me without my knowing it. I've got homework and books to read in my backpack. I'm seeing more of the school librarian now than I ever did before my parents turned up missing. Before I go upstairs I look out the kitchen window and see that the light is on in front of his shed. That either means he is out there or he forgot to turn it off. No way am I going out there to find out which it is.

I put the chair in front of my door and then take a quick bath, put on my pjs and my favorite pink robe, which I have worn just about every night for a year now. I move the bedside lamp closer so I can get the most out of its feeble light, lie down on my stomach, and breeze through my homework. Even the math problems are really no problem at all. Then I pull out one of the books I've borrowed. It's one that Ms. Shabbas once said I just had to read because you can really identify with the heroine and it takes you somewhere else. Which is where I want to be, for sure.

It turns out that she was right. The book truly does take my mind off things. Before I know it I've read a dozen chapters. I feel like I'm on a sailing ship with the heroine. Until I start wondering what Charlotte Doyle would do if she switched places with me. And I realize that I don't know what she would do any more than I know what I should do. I put a bookmark in to keep my place, lean back on my pillow, and close my eyes. As always, at least since I've been here, I don't turn out the light. I just want to rest my eyes. I don't want to go to sleep.

But I do.

And, instantly, I am there in that same dream. I'm back in the cave, the body of a partridge warm and limp in my hands. I'm holding it out to my uncle as he crouches in his corner. Without looking over his shoulder, he reaches an arm back. I see for the first time that his fingers are long and hairy and his fingernails are thick and sharp, more like claws. He grabs the dead bird so hard that I hear its bones crack.

"I thought it would be a rabbit," he growls. "Did you catch a rabbit?"

"No," I say. "This is all."

Then he begins to eat. I don't see him eat it, but I hear his teeth crunching through feathers and flesh and bones. He eats it all, growling as he swallows.

Then he reaches his arm back again. I stare at his fingers. A few small feathers from the partridge are stuck to them and the nails are red with blood.

"Hold out your arm, child," he says.

I don't give him my arm. Instead I hold out a stick the size of my wrist. His groping hand closes about it.

"Arrggh," he growls. "Even thinner and harder than before. No flesh at all, only bone. You must eat more, my niece. Eat and grow fat for me."

I sit up. I'm awake.

I say that aloud. "I'm awake. It was all a dream."

But then I look around me and I see this room—as bare and cold as the chamber of a cave. And then the *snick, snick, snick* of the locks.

No, it wasn't a dream.

6

No Pictures

HERE ARE NO PHOTOS at all in this house. No pictures of any kind, no paintings, not even any mirrors, aside from that small cloudy one in my bathroom. Even that was not up on the wall at first. I found it tucked behind the wardrobe and hung it up in the bathroom. Whenever I leave each day I take it off the bathroom wall and carefully put it in its original hiding place. I just have this feeling that if I don't do that, it will be gone when I come back. There is nothing else in this house to show his face or anyone else's.

When he picked me up, he smiled and laughed and talked like a concerned adult. It must have been an effort for him. His face was drawn and thin, angular with high cheekbones and a chin that jutted out, a high forehead with only a fringe of hair around his ears. But he looked human then.

As soon as he got me into the car, he started to change. I remember him putting on sunglasses and pulling his big hat down so that his face was concealed from me and from other drivers. I caught a glimpse of the side of his face every now and then, and it seemed as if the flesh was melting off his bones. At the time I figured the light was playing tricks on me, but now I'm not so sure. Ever since that day he's been careful not to show me his face at all. He always keeps his back to me.

And his hands! He'd kept them in his pockets, hidden from the social service people. But I could see them as they held the wheel. They were white, pale, pale white. And the skin on them was so thin that I thought I could see through to the bones. And the fingernails were thick and long and sharp like claws. He must have seen me looking because he slipped on a pair of leather gloves at the next stoplight. Then I turned away to watch the trees and telephone poles and the houses whizzing past, being left behind us as we went down that road toward someplace I never wanted to go.

He didn't speak much that day. He just opened the car door when we got to the house.

"Get out," he whispered.

I got out.

"Go in," he said.

I went in.

"Eat."

I ate the plate of food he put in front of me while he stood behind me and watched until I was done.

"Your room is upstairs," he said.

And I went up to it with my box and my suitcase, and he shut the door behind me and locked it. I remember wondering that night if the door would ever be unlocked again. I also remember not caring whether I lived or died. I missed my parents so much. And then I remember feeling zombielike and conking out.

I still miss them. But I can't believe that they're gone forever. Dad always told me that being a dreamer meant that I had a special kind of gift like our old people had long ago. If they really were never going to come back I'd know somehow through my dreams. But I haven't had that kind of dream. Instead, I just have this feeling that they're out there somewhere and that they will be back. And when they come back I will be there and they'll hug me and explain why they were gone and things will be all right again. I do care whether I live or die.

It is the middle of the night. It is still Wednesday night, a night that just doesn't seem to want to end, that just keeps creeping along. But my mind is moving like a runaway freight train. Run away, that's exactly what I feel like doing. But run away where? First of all I've got almost no money, and without it I wouldn't get far. He'd find me and bring me right back here.

But that is not the only reason I haven't run away. I have this feeling that if I'm ever going to see my mother and father again, I need to be here. That somehow my uncle is involved in their disappearance, even though he didn't show up until after they were gone.

Trust your dreams. Both my parents said

that. That's our old way, our Mohawk way. The way of our ancestors. Trust the little voice that speaks to you. That is your heart speaking. But when those feelings, those dreams, those voices are so confusing, what do you do then?

"Help," I whisper. "Help."

I'm not sure who I'm talking to when I say that, but I hope they're listening.

7

The Counselor

HEN THE MORNING COMES I haven't dreamed again. I haven't slept. I've been thinking about what I can do, and I've made up my mind. I've got a plan at last. It's a simple one, but simple ones are probably the best. It's also the only thing I can think to do.

At school you are always hearing about kids with problems. And there are people called counselors whose job is supposed to be to help kids who have them. It seems to me that most kids never actually see them. At our school, at least, the counselor is kept busy by the kids who are always in trouble or getting into trouble. Her name is Mrs. Rudder. Unless you are frothing at the mouth or something, it just isn't easy to get in to her.

As soon as I walk into the classroom I go right up to Ms. Shabbas. She doesn't do the adult thing of seeming to listen while not really hearing you because she thinks she already has the answer. She listens so well that she even forgets to sing whatever show tune she's picked out for that morning.

"It's gotten worse for me," I tell her. "It's driving me crazy. Every night when I hear him lock me in my room I think I'm going to scream."

Ms. Shabbas sits up straighter at that. "He locks you in? You didn't tell me about that before."

As soon as class goes out to rec, she takes me straight to the counselor's office. The door is partially open. I've walked by the door a million times and never gone in before. Ms. Shabbas pushes it open the rest of the way and pulls me in with her.

One whole wall to the left of the desk is taken up with pigeonholes. Not the kind that you put mail in, but smaller. Every one has the name of a kid written under it, and in every pigeonhole is a little pill bottle. Ritalin and stuff like that. The kids who need meds have to take their daily pill in Mrs. Rudder's office. There's a water cooler and paper cups, lots of them. On the other wall are some posters about not smoking and not taking drugs. I guess the two walls balance each other out.

"Can I help you?" says a voice from behind us that sounds like the person mostly wants to help us to leave.

We turn around and Mrs. Rudder is standing there. She's not very tall, but she has this way of looking at people that makes them feel as if they're being shrunk down under a microscope.

Ms. Shabbas, though, refuses to be diminished.

"Molly needs to talk to someone."

"I can make an appointment for . . ." Mrs. Rudder says, stepping past us to her desk and starting to look at her appointment book. "Now!" Ms. Shabbas says.

"I'm very busy," Mrs. Rudder replies. "I'm sure this can—"

"This child is afraid," Ms. Shabbas says.

"Look at her eyes." She won't take no for an answer.

The next thing I know, I'm sitting in the chair and Mrs. Rudder is leaning over her desk asking me questions and taking notes while Ms. Shabbas listens.

At first I can't make any headway. I'm telling the truth, but I feel like I'm not giving the right answers to the questions I am asked in a calm, matter-of-fact way.

"Has he ever touched you in a bad way?"

"No."

"Hmmm." Mrs. Rudder nods. "So he's never hit you?"

"No."

"Has he ever threatened you?"

"Not really."

"Ah-hah," Mrs. Rudder says. She looks over at Ms. Shabbas and shakes her head. I can tell that she thinks I am wasting her time. She's no longer sitting but standing up in a way that makes me feel as if I'll be standing up soon, on my way out her door. "What has he done that makes you afraid?"

I know what I want to say. I want to say that I see him looking at me out of the corner of his eye in a way that makes chills go down my back. Even when I'm walking down the hall and going into my room I feel like I'm still being looked at. It is as if eyes are watching me wherever I go in his house. I want to tell her that whenever he comes into a room, the air gets colder. Whenever I know he is thinking about me I have that feeling like someone is walking over my grave. I want to say that he's not really a human being, he is something else. I don't know what. He is fattening me up. But if I say that they'll suspect I'm nuts. I want to tell them about my dreams. But I know that if I tell Mrs. Rudder my dreams are warning me about the danger I'm in, she'll move from mere suspicion to absolute certainty that I'm lying.

Instead, I say the one thing that does get her attention.

"He locks me in my room at night."

Mrs. Rudder sits back down. She looks right at me over her desk, her hands clutched together. "Every night?"

"Every night."

"Can you come out if you ask?"

"I don't think so."

More things are said, but this was a big one. I see Ms. Shabbas nodding to me. Mrs. Rudder has listened. She'll do something.

But not much.

That afternoon Mrs. Rudder and a man who is introduced to me as Mr. Wintergreen from Child Welfare escort me to the house. Ms. Shabbas wanted to come along, but Mrs. Rudder told her that it wouldn't be following proper procedure.

He's waiting because they've called him on the phone an hour before we get there. Plenty of time for him to get ready. He's wearing his hat and a human face again and he smiles at them. They don't seem to notice that he doesn't offer to shake hands, that he keeps his hands in the pockets of his sweater.

"Your niece is very upset," Mrs. Rudder says to him.

"I understand," he says. "She's had a lot to deal with."

They follow him upstairs. He shows them the door to my room. There is no lock on the outside of the door. Never was. And no sign of screw holes that would be there if a lock had been removed. The only lock is on the inside. See, there's the release for the lock on the inside of the door, he tells them. Her side of the door. She can get out any time she wants.

"She's a very imaginative child," he adds.

I can't say anything. How can I say that he had time enough to change the door frame and the door? It wouldn't make any difference no matter what I said. They believe him, not me. I'm the melodramatic one. He's just a kindly older man who's taken in a difficult young relative.

They stand up. They're going to go and leave me there with him.

Mrs. Rudder leans over and places a hand on my shoulder. "Molly, dear," she says. "If you are still having these anxiety attacks, I can fit you into my calendar next week."

She looks up at my uncle and smiles. "Thank you for your time."

I hold my hand up as they walk toward the door as if to stop them. I want to scream, but I can't. They think I'm waving and they wave back to me as they go through the door, as it closes behind them, as my uncle goes over to the door and locks it.

As he turns, without looking at me, I wonder what he is going to say, what he is going to do . . .

But he doesn't say anything about it. It's as if he has no anger, no real emotions at all.

"Your dinner is in the refrigerator" is all he

says. Then he goes upstairs. I can hear the whirring of an electric screwdriver. I don't even have to guess what he's doing. After a while he comes down and walks out the back door to his work shed.

That night, when I am in my room and my door is closed, I hear his feet coming up the stairs. Then, after that moment of heart-stopping silence, there is the familiar sound. *Snick.* As he locks my door from the outside.

8

The Girl in the Story

I**T'S WORSE THAN IT WAS** before. Now he knows how I really feel about him. He knows that I suspect him. That means he'll be twice as watchful.

To calm myself, I try to imagine him sitting in front of his computer or out in his toolshed, a normal person doing normal things. But I can't. All I can see in my mind is the image of the cave creature from my dream crouched in the corner, its long, uncombed hair over its face, its clawed hand reaching backward to grasp my arm to see if I am fat enough to eat. I don't want to think about that.

I stretch out on the bed. It is all so hopeless. I try to remember one of the funny stories that Dad tells, ones in which the things that happen are so silly you just have to laugh. Some of them are old stories, but some are about things that happened to him when he was a kid, like the time when he talked his little brother into jumping into a muddy pond with all his clothes on to try to catch a turtle. Then, realizing his little brother was going to get into trouble because he'd gotten his clothes dirty, Dad jumped in, too, so that both of them would be in trouble. That way the trouble would be only half as bad for each of them, Dad explained. Maybe that doesn't sound funny to you, but the way Dad told it always made me laugh. Thinking about it I almost do laugh, until another thought comes to me. I may never hear my father's voice again. Then the little smile that had started to form on my face disappears.

I'm so sure that I won't be able to sleep that it surprises me when I realize I'm dreaming again. I am no longer in the room that has never been mine. Instead I am standing in a forest. I know I haven't gotten there by sleep-walking. Even if the door had been left unlocked and I'd found my way out of the house, I could never have found a place like this in the waking world. The trees are so big, bigger than the redwoods of California that I've seen in pictures. There haven't been trees that big around here in central New York for three hundred years or more.

The trees are not the only clue that I'm somewhere other than the usual waking world. The two figures who stand in front of me make it more than clear that I'm back in that dream. One of them is the same rabbit I saw before. It's a snowshoe rabbit. It wears its summer coat of brown, not the white of winter that it puts on when the snow is on the ground. It's more than twice as big as the little cottontail rabbits that I sometimes see at the edge of the school play-ground by the little patch of woods.

The other one is me. How strange to be me, looking at me. I blink twice at that. But there are subtle differences. The other me has skin that is a little more tanned than mine. Her hair is longer, and there is a little scar on her cheek, just below her left eye, as if something sharp—a knife or a claw—cut across it once. She is also dressed the way I remember being dressed in my dream of the cave. Moccasins, deerskin dress, braided rawhide bracelet on her wrist. I stare at that bracelet. I remember my mother telling me about bracelets like that that Mohawk children used to wear to make sure they woke up safely from their dreams.

I blink my eyes again and the other me is gone. Or is she? I'm standing next to the rabbit now. There are moccasins on my feet, there's a rawhide bracelet around my wrist, and I'm wearing her deerskin dress . . . my deerskin dress.

"I'm in someone else's story," I blurt out.

"No, Little Sister," says a kind voice at my feet. "It is not someone else's story."

I look down at the rabbit. "What?" I say.

"This is your story now," the rabbit continues. "But even though it is your story, you are not safe. You must be brave. Your spirit must still remain strong."

For some reason, that makes me angry. After all that's happened I don't need some furry Oprah Winfrey to tell me I need to get my spiritual act in order.

"Is that all you've got to say?" I ask the

rabbit, clenching my fists. "That I'm in trouble? Don't you think I know that?"

The rabbit hops close to me and places its front paws on my feet as it looks up at me.

"Little Sister," it says, "I am here to tell you something."

"What?" I ask in a voice that is no longer angry, a voice that is small and halting.

"Your parents," the rabbit says, "they have been buried."

"No," I whisper. "They can't be dead." I want to shout, but to do that I'd have to catch my breath, and right now it feels as if I can't breathe at all.

The rabbit's paws are patting my knee.

"Little Sister," the rabbit says, "I did not say they were dead. If they were dead, then you could not help them. They are buried but not dead."

Buried but not dead? Can I find hope in that? And if I can't understand what it means, how can I help them? I'm confused and I want to ask the rabbit to explain, but before I can do so it is gone.

I sit up, looking around for the rabbit, reaching for it . . . and I find myself grasping the blankets of my bed.

9

Pictures

I WAS INTERVIEWED TODAY by a bunch of people. The nurse, the school psychologist, Mrs. Rudder. They think my problem may be a chemical one and that I need counseling. They think that my story about my uncle was brought on by the stress of uncertainty combined with my already imaginative personality. Lucky I didn't tell them about the rabbit dream.

Ms. Shabbas talks with me after school about it all.

"If you ask me, witch doctors know more about people than some of these professionals," she says. "If there's a problem, throw a prescription at it. That's all they seem to know lately."

I wonder why she is talking to me this way. I don't think most teachers would. But Ms. Shabbas is not most teachers. When she likes someone, trusts someone, she really talks to them. I've never realized before how much she likes me.

"Honey," she says, "I don't care if they didn't find any lock on your door. My bones tell me something's rotten in the state of Denmark. We got trouble right here in River City. *Comprende?*"

I nod. Part of me wants to jump up and down, pump my fist into the air, and yell, "Yes!" But even though I have an ally now, there may not be much she can do. Plus I'm still sick— and confused—about what I heard in my dream, those words the rabbit said. My parents are buried.

"Listen," Ms. Shabbas whispers, breaking

into my thoughts. "I'm not saying do anything stupid. But bring me something solid to make your case, I'll move heaven and earth to get you away from that man. Just be careful, hear me?"

"I will," I say. But I am also thinking that it may not matter whether I am careful or not. Tomorrow is Friday. Whenever I think of that, I start feeling even more scared.

I'm the last one to get onto the bus. The driver's not happy that he had to wait for me, but Ms. Shabbas called down and told him to hold on till I got there. A truck pulls up behind the bus as I get on. Men climb out carrying toolboxes and equipment like drills, power saws, big wrenches, and cable cutters. The school is being hooked up to the information superhighway. They'll be here again tomorrow, then finish after the weekend. The weekend that begins tomorrow afternoon.

By the time I get to the house, I am just about overcome by a feeling of dread. It doesn't help that the days are getting much shorter now and it is almost dark already. As I open the door and go inside, a little shiver goes down my spine.

"Hello," I call. No one answers. I look into the kitchen. No note telling me to eat. I wonder if something is wrong, something more wrong than usual, I should say. I walk back into the hall and I notice that the door to my uncle's study is open. It is rarely open and it draws me, like a moth to a flame. Step by step I walk down the hall. I'm trying to stop myself, but I can't. The only thing I seem to be able to do is go more slowly so that my steps don't make the floor creak like it would if I went faster. I try to walk the way my father taught me that our Mohawk ancestors would when they wanted to go through the forest without making any noise. My elbows close to my sides, my hands held in front of me, I place one foot down slowly, then another until I reach the study door.

It's a small room. My uncle isn't in there; there's no place he could hide. His chair is pushed back from the desk as if he suddenly had to go somewhere. I can see, though, the one window at the back of the room out into the yard. The toolshed door is open and a light is coming out of it. That must be it. For some reason he had to get up and go out to the shed to do something.

I should turn around now. I should not go into that room. But I still do.

There's a color laser printer next to the computer, the kind that does really high-quality prints on heavy glossy paper. Just like regular photographs. But what attracts my attention are the three small TV monitors on the shelf above the computer. I take another step closer and I freeze.

I feel as if I have been kicked in the stomach. I'm unable to move. My mouth is open and I think I'm about to scream. But I don't. Instead I will myself to thaw out, tell my feet to start moving me out of that room before my uncle comes back. I get up the stairs. I'm just opening the door to my room when I hear the front door open.

"Where are you?" my uncle calls. His raspy voice is a little out of breath, maybe a little worried. "Where are you?" he calls again, louder this time.

"Up here," I call back. "I don't feel good. I'm going to bed."

His heavy feet are coming up the stairs faster than usual. I shut the door before he gets to me.

He's breathing hard, waiting outside in the hall. He doesn't speak and neither do I. Finally, he snicks the lock and goes back downstairs. I crouch in the corner of the room with my arms around my legs. All I can see, even when I close my eyes, are the pictures on those TV screens. Live pictures from the hidden cameras trained on the front door, the back door, and the door to my room.

10

Looking

VEN THOUGH I'M more afraid than I've
ever been, I'm thinking fast as I crouch
in the corner curled into a ball, hoping
I'm out of sight of the cameras. I have so many
questions in my mind. When did he set up
those TV cameras and why haven't I seen
them? Why does he have them set up like that?
Then there is the scariest question of all. What
will he do next?

I've got to be logical, though. That is what
Mom always tells me. Think first before you try
to run away from a problem, otherwise you

might run right into an even worse one. And stay alert.

I've always been a light sleeper. Dad used to say it was because I had warrior genes and he'd tease me about it, calling me Warrior Girl. He told me my Indian name might be Keeps Herself Awake. In the old days I would have been the one told to keep watch at night against enemies. Neither he nor Mom could ever come into my room at night without my waking up instantly.

There is no way that my so-called uncle can sneak into my room without my knowing it. Unless I've been drugged. But I haven't felt strange since that first night. I've stayed away from the food. I'm certain now that the person who calls himself my uncle is an impostor at best, and something much more terrible at worst. I begin to think of my dream, of the similarities between the creature fattening up the girl and my uncle. Skeleton Man. He's a modern-day Skeleton Man and this house is his cave. A glimmer of hope appears to me. If it really is like my dream, maybe I can find an answer in my dreams about what to do.

It is too cold in the corner and it's hard to think there. I get up and climb on the bed and let my head fall back onto the pillow. I start remembering back to the times I've come awake in the night since I've been here. Lots of times, now that I think of it. And every time it's been because I've had the feeling that I've been watched. I've just opened one eye, slowly, just a little. Not enough for anyone to notice I'm no longer sleeping. My whole body has been awake and waiting to act each time I've done this. But I've never seen anything. There has never been anyone else in my room. Never. But maybe there's a TV camera set up to look at me in here, too. Maybe the monitor for that camera is in his bedroom down the hall.

I look up at the ceiling. Up there is where it must be. We've learned about fiber optics in school and I know just how small the opening can be for a lens. No more than a pinhole. There's a light fixture right over my head. I'm betting that is where it is. If I piled my suitcase and my box on my bed and climbed up on top of them, I could probably reach it. The ceiling is only about eight feet high. But I won't do that now. I don't want him to know that I know. This has to be like a chess match. Never let your opponent know what your next move will be until you make it.

I think of what Dad taught me about chess. He loves the game and is always coaxing me to play it with him. Chess is a game based on war, on two armies starting out equal and trying to wipe each other out. Not with brute force, but with strategy, with thinking ahead much farther than one move.

My so-called uncle probably doesn't think of this as chess or any kind of an equal contest. He probably thinks that he has all the weapons. He's just playing with me.

But if I think of this as a chess game, it gives me an advantage. I can't just be a victim. I have to counter, even find some way to attack. Great, I think. But now what will my move be? I know that I have to make one. And it has to be a good one. Something my dad said comes back to me, some of the Mohawk warrior wisdom he was always teaching me. "It doesn't matter if you are the hunted or the hunter. Sometimes the most important thing you can do in a tough situation is to keep quiet, breathe slowly, and think."

So that is what I do—sit quietly for a long time. Finally, I think I know what to do.

First of all, I don't take off my clothes. I just slip off my sneakers and socks and crawl under the sheets. I pull the blanket over my head like a tent. I know it isn't any real protection, but it makes me feel safe. It is like when I was a little kid and used to make pretend longhouses under card tables draped with curtains. No one could see me.

"Help me," I whisper as I settle down to sleep. And this time it's not just a generalized plea to the universe. I'm speaking to my dreams.

11

Running

S I HIDE UNDER the covers, I feel as if I am never going to go to sleep. The thought that eyes might be watching me, that a camera might be looking down from overhead makes me as tense as a guitar string about to be plucked. I close my eyes tight against that thought and I clench my fists. I'm not just scared; I'm also angry and frustrated. How am I ever going to fall asleep?

Suddenly the covers are whisked away from

me. I jump up with a yell. I'm ready to resist however I can. I'll kick and bite and scratch. Even though my so-called uncle is bigger than I am, I won't give up without a fight. I blink my eyes, trying to bring the shadowy world into focus, step back with my hands still held up . . . and bump into something big and hard and rough. I spin around and find myself face-to-face with the trunk of a giant tree.

A tree? How did a tree get into the room? And, for that matter, where has the room gone?

"Little Sister," says a voice from behind me. It is not a human voice. Yet it is a voice I welcome. I know who it is even before I turn around.

As I do, I realize that I'm back in deerskin clothing with moccasins made of thick moose hide.

"Little Sister!" the rabbit says again. This time it sounds as impatient as a parent trying to get the wandering attention of a child.

"Yes," I say.

"You must keep running," the rabbit says. It points with its left paw toward a direction that I somehow know to be the direction of the sunrise. "The one who seeks to devour you is close on our trail. Follow me."

The rabbit begins to run and I follow close behind. I've only taken a few steps when a scream splits the night. It is so terrible—and so close—that I stumble. But I don't fall. I just run harder. The rabbit is leading me though the dark forest. There is just enough light from the moon, her face like that of a grandmother trying to help her little ones see their way.

She isn't just lighting *our* way, though. I can hear heavy feet thudding behind us. We run and run. We run through a glade of great pine and cedar trees and down a hill into a ravine thick with brush. We force our way through tangles of saplings and blackberry bushes. We leap over fallen logs, splash through a swamp thick with ferns, climb one hill and then another. How long we run, I don't know. I seem to be able to run without getting winded as I would in the waking world. But we are not getting away. The heavy feet keep thudding behind us.

Then I begin to hear something else. It is water. The rabbit leads me headlong down a trail that looks familiar to me. I've been in this place before, not in my dreams but in the waking world. I can tell by the giant stones and the lake that glitters in the valley off to our right and the shape of the land. It's the park where my father and mother used to take me sometimes on picnics. It's only about two miles from the house of my so-called uncle. But things are different. In the waking world there are roads and sidewalks and benches. Here there are only old tall trees and a deer trail. Still, I know where we're going. Toward the river just above the big waterfall.

Moonlight gleams on the river just ahead of us as we begin to scramble down a steep slope. The river is high, higher than I've ever seen it before. But the swinging suspension bridge that I've always loved, the bridge I've crossed so many times, is not there. Of course it's not there, a voice inside me says. This is long ago, even if it isn't far away.

But if there is no bridge, how are we going to get across the river?

We're right on the bank now, and the rabbit stops. It stands up to its full height, looking one way and then the other, as if confused. Did it expect a bridge here, too? What kind of spirit guide is the rabbit, anyhow?

"What can we—" I start to say. But I don't finish my question. The howl that rips apart the night air is so loud, so full of hunger, that it

makes me spin around and fall to one knee.

The creature is there, on top of the slope above us. He's no more than a hundred yards away from us, and the light of the moon that shone so gently on me is stark and hard in the way it lights up the creature that looms there above me. He is taller than a tall man. He wears tattered buckskin clothing, clothing that hangs from him in shreds. But he has no need of clothing to warm his flesh, for whatever flesh he once had is gone. Shiny white bones can be seen through the rips in his buckskin shirt, and his head is a glistening skull.

But even though he is a skeleton, he has eyes. His eyes are green and burn like strange flames, and there is a darkness about his teeth that I'm sure is dried blood. The creature turns his head, as if sniffing the air. Then he stares down toward us and he opens his mouth in a wide grin. He raises his arm and points down toward us. Correction, toward me. For when I look around for my guide, I realize that the rabbit has disappeared,

"My niece," the Skeleton Man cries, in a voice that is both scream and whisper, "I am coming for youuuuu!"

I'm ready, more than ready, to wake up now.

12

Across the Log

A S THE SKELE-
ton Man
starts down
the hill toward me,
he seems to have a
hard time keeping his
balance on the steep
slope. Waving his long
arms, he begins to
slide. His bony feet
are too slippery! He
begins to fall and
then, crashing
through the brush and
fallen limbs, he rolls right past me
and splashes into the river.

"We have to keep running," says a voice
next to me. I look down. It's the rabbit.

"Where were you?" I ask. I'm really

upset that it deserted me.

"I knew the creature would fall." the rabbit says. "That is why I took us down this trail. But he has not been killed. He will climb out of the river again and follow us. Hurry, I have found the place where we can get across."

The rabbit starts up a trail I hadn't noticed before. We climb higher and higher. A roaring sound is getting louder and louder. Then I realize what I am hearing, and I know where we are. We're going up toward the top of the falls where the river is narrower. There is another bridge there in my time, one that a road goes over. But what will be there now?

I am panting hard when we reach the top of the steep trail.

"Oh no," I say as I see what we have to cross.

"Oh yes," says the rabbit.

I look hard at the rabbit, for it sounds as if it's making fun of me. But all it does is keep pointing with its paw toward the place where we must go. There is nothing more than a dead tree that has fallen across the river, right over the falls. Even though the tree was tall enough to reach the other side, its trunk isn't that thick. Going across will be like walking on a tightrope.

The moonlight glistens on the white foam of the water striking the rocks far below. It is a long way down. I've heard that when you fall in a dream you always wake up before you hit the bottom. I don't want to find out if this is true. I also have a feeling that this dream isn't just any dream. If I get hurt in this dream, I think it won't just be a scary memory when I wake up—if I wake up.

I want to protest again, but there's no time. The rabbit is already halfway across and I know that I have to follow. I've never been afraid of heights. After all, I'm the daughter of a Mohawk man who worked the high iron before he went into the banking business and met my mom. My dad and other Mohawks like him built places like the World Trade towers. But even though I'm not usually afraid of heights, I've never done anything like this before. Maybe, I think, I could crawl across. I stand there, not ready to put even one foot on that tree trunk.

"Ayyyyy-aaaahhhh!"

The scream is now so close that I am on the log before I have time to decide whether to go over it upright or on my stomach with my legs wrapped around it. I don't walk across, I run!

Maybe it is foolish to turn around to look, but when I do I see I was almost too slow. Skeleton Man is there, standing on the other bank, one bony foot already on the log. He holds out his arm and points at me.

"My niece," he whispers, "I am coming for you."

The rabbit nudges my leg with its paw.

"Don't run now," the rabbit says. "Wait."

Skeleton Man is coming across the log now, taking one step at a time, his eyes boring into mine. I feel as if I'm being hypnotized, but I can't let that happen. I know what I have to do. Another step and I still wait, another step, another, and now he is in the middle. I tear my eyes away from him, go down onto one knee, and push the end of the log as hard as I can.

"Noooo!" Skeleton Man howls.

But he is too late. The end of the log slips off the bank into the water, twists as the current catches it, and then goes tumbling over the falls, carrying Skeleton Man with it toward the sharp rocks below.

I open my eyes before he hits the bottom. It was all a dream, the whole thing. I'm safe in my bed and it's morning, and I feel great. I can see a crack of light coming in through the closed curtains. I jump out of bed and throw open the curtain, certain that I'll see my mom's autumn flower bed with its birdbaths and feeders, my old swing set, and the little willow tree Dad and I planted.

But the morning sunlight doesn't show me that at all. My heart sinks again as I see below me a dreary backyard where nothing wants to grow and the tall, bent-shouldered shape of my uncle walking toward his toolshed. I step back from the window before he can catch a glimpse of me and I sit down on the floor. Nothing has changed.

I get up and go into the small bathroom. I try not to even think about the possibility of another camera being in there, but just in case, I keep a big towel wrapped around me as I wash up and get dressed.

13

Tomorrow

As I walk into Ms. Shabbas's classroom, she gives me a very big smile and mouths the words, "We'll talk later."

I nod to her and smile. The door to my room was unlocked this morning after all, just like every other morning. Breakfast was waiting for me on the table. A blue bowl with cornflakes in it, a glass of milk, and a smaller glass of orange juice—all so neatly laid out that it looked like something in one of those old situation comedies about happy families that they rerun on cable. Except no mother and father. My so-called uncle was nowhere to be seen. I sat down just like a normal kid. Then I looked around furtively in every direction and shoved all of the food into my backpack.

And now I'm safe in school. Everything is like it always is here. The only thing different is the workmen. They're sloppy, leaving their tools all over the place. And here I am in my own classroom, a place so safe-feeling that it is unreal to me. I look around, blinking my eyes to make sure I'm not imagining it.

Will Ms. Shabbas believe me when I tell her about my seeing those television monitors? Or about the camera I think may be hidden in my light fixture? Will that make me sound ultra-paranoid or what? I know she's on my side and I want to tell her. But then I also know what the rabbit told me in my dream about my parents being buried and that I have to save them. If I tell Ms. Shabbas about the cameras, she'll take me away and then I won't be able to save them. Somehow I feel that I have to do it by myself.

Today Ms. Shabbas doesn't forget to sing. It's that song about Annie that I sang myself to sleep with. "Tomorrow." She looks right at me as she sings about how it is going to be better on the day after this one. I know she is telling me that she is still on my side, that I have to buck up, keep a stiff upper lip, not give up the ship. She loves songs and stories that have upbeat endings. Mention the *Titanic* to most people and they think of a tragic love story. Mention it to Ms. Shabbas and she will start belting out something from *The Unsinkable Molly Brown*. Molly, just like me. Except I am not named for some survivor of a shipwreck. I'm named Molly after Molly Brant, a Mohawk warrior woman from the eighteenth century. "Back during the American Revolution," my mom told me, "one word from Molly Brant went farther than a thousand words from any white man. No one ever got the best of Molly Brant."

For some weird reason, Ms. Shabbas and her up-with-people singing helps me. Corny-but-sincere is her style, and it is just what I need this morning. I want to get out of my seat and walk up and hug her while she is singing. Instead I just give her a thumbs-up sign when she is done. She winks at me.

But when the time comes for us to talk, I still don't tell her anything. I need her to be on my side, and I'm too scared she won't believe me. Nothing new, I say. Which is true. It's just that now I know my so-called uncle has been keeping watch on me through a camera lens.

"Will you be okay over the weekend, honey?"

The weekend starts tonight. Every kid in America but me is looking forward to the weekend. I have a feeling that whatever awful thing he has in store for me is going to happen tomorrow. I swallow hard and make myself smile.

"I'll be fine," I say.

"Should I come over and check in on you?"

"If you have time."

"I'll make time on Sunday."

And that is how we leave it. She will call my so-called uncle after school and let him know she is going to come over to visit on Sunday. She's going to take me out for lunch and a visit to the park. If nothing else, it will let him know that someone is watching and that he won't get away with it.

But the small measure of relief I feel is short-lived. Maybe, I think, he doesn't care if he gets away with it. If he is crazy or evil, maybe getting caught wouldn't bother him. If he gets caught after doing whatever he plans to do to me, that won't help me much, will it?

Sunday. That leaves all of tonight and all of tomorrow and tomorrow night. Sunday may be too late for me.

14

Toolshed

WHEN THE SCHOOL day ends, I hang back from the crowd of kids who head out the door. They're happy about the weekend. For them the clock's hands have been almost standing still, while for me they've been going double time. Like my brain is going around and around like a top that's out of control. But it has kept circling back to one idea. It is a crazy one, but the only one I've been able to come up with.

Like the kids, the workmen have been eager for the day to end, too. They've even left before us. That's my first real break, that and the fact that they've left their toolboxes open again. Sure, they put a yellow ribbon across the hall in front of the library to keep people out. You know how easy it is to duck under a yellow ribbon? And though my backpack is a lot heavier when I get onto the bus, no one notices.

When I get off the bus, I stand for a long time looking down the darkening road. I feel so scared. I should run away now. But where? And what good would it do me? Not only that, but for some reason I feel as if running away now won't just affect me, but my whole family. My real family.

Dinner is waiting on the table for me. It's pizza, and it looks good and smells even better. And there's an open bottle of Coca-Cola, too. My favorite drink. I sit down and look at the pizza and then I shake my head. I won't eat any of this dinner, either.

"What's wrong?" My so-called uncle's whispery voice comes suddenly from behind me and it makes me jump. I turn and see him in the doorway, standing with his back to me. "Feeling sick again?" he says. There is a tone to his voice that worries me. It isn't concern; it's sarcasm. It is like he is saying that he knows more than I do, that he knows what is going to happen and I don't. I hope he is wrong.

"I'm just tired," I answer.

I take my bag and go upstairs and go into the room and lock the door. I take a book out of my bag and try to read it. The letters of the words all look like strange insects crawling over the page. But time doesn't crawl by. Before long it is dark outside. I turn out the light in the room and wait.

His footsteps come up the stairs and pause for a long time, too long, in front of the door. When the snick of the outside lock comes, I start breathing again. I stuff the pillows under the covers to make it look like I'm in there. I crouch in the shadowiest corner by the window. I start counting the times I breathe in and out. I am up to three thousand four when I hear the sound of the door downstairs. Yes, I think. It's just as I hoped. He's keeping to the same routine he follows every night. He always spends time in that toolshed before he comes up and goes to bed. I peek out the lower corner window and see his shadowy shape cross the yard and the light go on in his toolshed.

My feet don't want to move. "Now," I say to them. With small, timid steps I make my way over to my backpack, open it, and fish around for what I want, a heavy thing with a pistol grip. I pull it out. A power screwdriver. The door may be locked, but the hinges are on the inside.

The whirring of the drill sounds terribly loud, even though I keep telling myself it isn't. I stop everything and listen. I don't hear anything and I continue. One screw, two, three. The screws are long and heavy, and I put each one into my pocket as it comes out. I have to get up on my toes to reach the top ones. I drop the fifth screw and it hits the floor with a loud *thwack*. Again I stop work and listen. But all I hear is silence. I start breathing once more.

Finally the last screw is removed. I stand up and take the foot-long crowbar from my pack. I pry it between the jamb and the door. The door pops free with a soft *thump*. I grab hold and pull it toward me, and the locks slip out. Now that it is free on both sides, the door almost falls over, but I lean my shoulder against it and manage to prop it against the doorjamb. I slip out and pull my pack out after me. I can't get the door exactly back into place where it

was, but by leaning it a little I make it look like it is still closed.

I should have looked out the window before I left the room to see if light was showing under the toolshed door. But it is too late for that now. I put the pack over my shoulder and then start down the stairs, stepping sideways on each stair to try to keep them from creaking. It takes me a year to reach the bottom.

Now I'm only a few steps from the front door. But that is not where I am heading. I need evidence. I head for the room with the computer in it. There has to be something in there that I can take and use as proof, proof that my uncle isn't who he says he is, proof that I really am in danger.

The door is open again and that same light is shining from the computer screen. But I don't focus on that. Instead I turn to the pile of glossy pages next to the keyboard. I turn one over and it almost makes my heart stop beating. It is a photo of my mother. And it is not an old picture but a recent one. How do I know that? Because she is wearing the same brand-new blouse she was wearing the last day I saw her and Dad go out the door. But she doesn't look exactly the same as she did on that day. On that day she didn't have her hands tied together and she wasn't leaned back against the rough board wall of a shed and she didn't have a piece of duct tape over her mouth.

15

Hard Evidence

I STOP LOOK-
ing at pic-
tures after
finding the one
of my mother.
Things are start-
ing to make more
sense and no sense
at all. All I know is
that I have to take the
whole stack of pictures
from his computer desk. I put them into the
folder in my backpack. There's other stuff on
his desk, too. Lists of things that have to do with
databases and hacking into computers like the
one at the bank where Dad works. I grab that
stuff and then add a handful of computer disks
lying on the desk. I zip the pocket tight and put
the backpack over my shoulder. Once I get rid

of the tools it won't be that heavy to carry. But I don't take out the rest of the tools I've borrowed from school. Not yet. I kneel down and make sure that my sneakers are tied and double knotted. I'm not going to change my plan about getting to the outside phone booth near the park entrance where I can call Ms. Shabbas, but I am going to add one thing to it.

I walk out the back door toward the toolshed. I've looked at that yard so many times from my window, but I've never been in it before. It is his place and he told me to stay away from it. Not that he needed to. Until now I've tried to avoid anyplace where he might be.

There are decorative stones on the ground that used to be part of the abandoned overgrown garden. They are white and round and the size of golf balls. I pick up three of them. I'm a good runner, maybe the best in the school, but I'm no pitcher. I might miss on the first throw.

But I don't. The stone sails through my upstairs window with a crash that is as satisfying to me as it is loud. I don't need to throw another stone. He's heard it, and he comes out of the toolshed moving so fast that it scares me. He doesn't move like an old man but like some

kind of big cat. He looks in all directions and seems to be sniffing the air. But he doesn't see me or smell me hiding behind the cedar bush next to the shed. He stares at the house and then lopes across the yard and goes inside.

I'm counting under my breath as I dart into the toolshed. When I get to a hundred, I tell myself, I'll turn and run no matter what. It is so clean and neat inside, the shelves are spotless, the tools hung on Peg-Boards. It's mechanical. It doesn't look as if a human being has ever been in here. Ten, eleven, twelve. I see that the back wall is at a funny angle. I try to push it and it moves like a door and then sticks. Thirteen, fourteen, fifteen. I pull out the crowbar and pry it open. There's a small room behind it with a dirt floor. But its not just dirt. In the middle of the floor is something that looks like a ring. Twenty-two, twenty-three. I kneel by the ring, brush dirt away, and see that it is connected to a trapdoor that is held shut by a hinged metal strap that fits over a thick metal staple. I pull out the pin that holds it shut. Then I take a deep breath and pull on the ring. The door is heavy, but it slowly begins to move. Dirt hisses off as I lift it. There's another door, a metal grating fastened with a padlock. But I can look down through it into the dark room hollowed out like a cave under the toolshed.

"Hello," I hiss. Twenty-seven, twenty-eight.

A hand reaches up to touch the grating. I recognize that hand.

"Dad," I whisper. Our fingers touch, link briefly before he falls back. My heart is pounding. It's really him! He's alive. There's so much I want to say, but I can't make my voice come out. And in the back of my mind I remember that I must keep counting. Thirty-one, thirty-two, thirty-three. I swallow the lump in my throat and manage to ask the question that I have to ask, even if I'm afraid of what the answer might be.

"Where's Mom?"

"She's here," he answers. His fingers push mine away. "Run."

"Is she all right? Are you all right?"

"Run, Molly," he says again. "There's no time. Get away!"

"No, Dad, not yet," I whisper. And as I say it I feel a certainty and strength like I've never felt before. I know what I have to do and I am going to do it.

I've got the bolt cutter out now. I maneuver it around to the lock that holds the grating and press down with all my strength. The jaws of the bolt cutter shear through the steel, as if it was butter. Fifty-seven, fifty-eight, fifty-nine.

"Run," Dad says again. "Now!"

"The falls, Dad," I whisper. "You know the place."

I push the bolt cutter and every other tool I have in my bag through the grating. I've lost count now. I don't know if there's enough time. I'm sure that by now he will have gone upstairs to my room. But the way he moved like a cat, so fast, makes me uncertain now how long he'll take.

I'm through the hidden door, the door of the toolshed is ahead of me. But I don't go through it straight. I duck and twist as I come out, and it's a good thing because he is there waiting in the darkness and he almost grabs me. His bony fingers slip through the loose braid in my hair. I scream and yank and I'm free. I go around the house toward the road. Just as I expected, he has gone around the other side to cut me off. He thinks I'm going to run toward town, toward other houses because his is the last house on the road. He's wrong. I'm going the other way, running fast. Running and running.

I venture a quick look back to see where he

is. He isn't far behind me, no more than fifty yards. The moonlight glitters off his white forehead. Suddenly a rabbit darts out of the bushes and crosses in front of him, making him stumble. I gain another twenty yards, running and running. Looking back will only slow me down. I won't risk that again. I feel the strength of that story from long ago in my legs. I won't get tired.

I run and run and keep running. I have gone at least a mile now. The lake glitters in the moonlight off to my right and the Visitors' Center is just ahead of me, but there's no time now to use the phone. I pass the sign for the park, turn onto the trail, and begin to climb. I can no longer hear him behind me. This is my territory now. I'm sure I know it better than the one chasing me.

But I don't. I round the corner where the trail is narrow and the cliff falls off to the right. He is there ahead of me, cutting me off. There is a grin on his skeletal face, and his long arms are spread wide as if in welcome.

16

Escape

OU CAN'T
escape me,"
he says in a
hollow voice, a
taunting voice. "Can
you, little niece?"

If I try to answer
him, I'll be done for. It
would be like a mouse
trying to argue with an
owl. Instead I throw my backpack at him and, as he staggers back a
step, I scramble up the slope off the trail
into the brush. The trail edge is thick with
blackberry bushes. They scratch at my hands
and my face. Dead thorns stick through my
jeans into my knees. But I get low, as low as a
rabbit, and I crawl through and under the
brush.

He can't. I hear him being held back by the thorny branches. I crawl until I find a clear area, then I stand up and move as quickly as I can along the dark, wooded slope. I roll my feet as I step like Dad taught me so that I don't make much sound. Then I stop and listen. I don't hear anything for a few heartbeats and then . . .

"Whooooo!" It's like the cry of an owl just below me on the trail. But it's not an owl, even though it makes me want to jump like a little mouse being scared out of hiding. "Whoooo!" Skeleton Man calls again. "I'm waiting for youuu. I will get youuuuuuu."

I don't move. I'll sit here all night if I have to. I won't let him scare me into showing myself. Silence. Nothing but silence for a long time. Too much silence, for it means that other things in the woods that would normally be making noise at this time know something is still out there. Something dangerous. Like me, they're waiting.

Then I see it. A beam of light coming through the forest. It is sweeping back and forth, not at random but moving slowly, patiently. He has a flashlight. Its illumination is moving toward me, its beam like the strand of a spider's web that will catch me. It's getting too close, and I have to move. I crawl downslope as slowly as I can, a hand's width at a time, until I reach the trail. Then I'm up and running toward the falls again. I'm not making much noise, but I begin to hear the feet of Skeleton Man thumping on the hard-packed earth of the trail behind me.

"Whoooo," he cries. "Whooooooo. I'm coming for youuuuuu!"

There's a place just ahead of us, around the next corner, where I remember my father and I had to duck under the long, low limb of a maple tree that overhung the trail. I'm praying that no one has trimmed that branch as the path bends around the hill. Yes! The branch is leaning over the narrow trail just as I'd remembered. I grab it as I run and it bends with me. Still holding it, I turn slightly. He's too close! He's about to grab me, but when I fall back and let the branch go, his hand misses me. The branch whips back to strike him in the face, knocking him off balance onto one knee and onto the loose stones at the steep edge of the trail. He begins to slip, and for a moment, it seems as if he is going to slide all the way off the trail into the deep ravine below. But, at the last moment, he whips one bony arm out, grabs the branch, and starts to pull himself back up. Before he can get to his feet I'm up and running again.

As I run I startle something that had been hiding in the brush next to the path. It runs ahead of me, clearly visible in a band of moonlight shining through the overhanging branches. It's a rabbit again. I know there are rabbits all through the park. You hardly ever walk through here in the morning or early evening without seeing at least four or five of them. It's not at all likely that it is the same one that slowed down my pursuer back near the house. But something in me tells me different, tells me that it's the same rabbit and it is trying to help me. It runs ahead of me and then suddenly darts off the main path onto a smaller, even steeper trail.

I know where this trail leads. It might seem like a dead end to some people if they just read the signs that say TRAIL CLOSED and BRIDGE OUT on them. But I can see that the wooden-planked suspension bridge over the gorge is still there. Its boards are old, but it should be able to hold my weight. I follow the rabbit up that trail, my feet slipping on the loose stones, my hands grasping at branches and clumps of grass as I climb.

Just as I'd remembered, there is a hole in the bottom of the chain-link fence big enough to crawl through. It was probably made by the local kids who carried up the narrow pieces of plywood to lay over the spots in the long, swaying bridge where the boards have rotted and fallen away, down into the stream, which is nothing more than a thin band of silver among the jagged rocks far below. But it doesn't look as if even the daredevil kids from the high school have ventured across the bridge for a long time.

I drop to my knees and crawl under the fence. A sharp piece of wire scratches my cheek and I feel the blood flow down my face. Another wire catches on my pant leg and I pull as hard as I can. I can't be caught here.

"WHOOO!" The eerie scream comes from right behind me and then there is a crash as his headlong rush takes him right into the chain-link wire. I feel something grabbing at my foot. I pull free, leaving my sneaker behind.

There's no time to stop or think. I start across the bridge, my arms spread out to hold the rusty cables on each side, my eyes looking down to see where to place my feet. One step, two, three. Old boards creak under my feet and the bridge begins gently swaying back and forth. Four, five, six. The rhythm is almost like that of a dance. Nine, ten, eleven, twelve, and I'm almost halfway across.

"Molly." The harsh whisper that cuts through the night from behind me makes me take a wrong step. My foot goes right through a rotten board. He's never spoken my name before, and the chill that it sends down my spine makes me shake all over. "Come back here."

I can't stop myself. I turn around and look. He's standing there, back at the end of the bridge, perhaps hesitant to cross it. His long arms are held up above his head, his fingers spread out so wide that they look like the talons of a giant bird. The moonlight glistens off his pale hard face and the top of his head, and it seems as if there is no skin at all. His eyes are twin blue flames burning from within his skull.

"No," I say, not just to him, but to myself. I wrench my foot free, break away from his hyp-notic gaze, and start forward again. There's a thin piece of plywood just ahead spanning the last ten feet.

Suddenly the bridge starts to shake. I know that he is on it, moving across to catch me. And he's coming fast. I'm on the plywood now and it bends, almost to the point where the end that overlaps the concrete lip at the end of the bridge slips free. But it doesn't. I reach the safety of the other side. Then I keep myself from doing the one thing I want to do—which is to scream for help and run headlong, run as fast as I can to get away from the bony hands that I know are about to reach out and grab me. Instead, I turn and drop down onto the ground and kick my heels against the edge of the piece of plywood. And even though he's already on it, the plywood slips—*fwap!*—past the lip of stone.

The plywood falls from beneath him, sails down into the gorge like a flipped playing card. He pitches forward, his long fingers clawing forward wildly. I try to pull myself back, but one clawing hand wraps around my ankle. It holds on so hard that I feel a searing pain, as if I'm being burned by those fingers. I begin to slide back toward the edge. I'm about to be pulled into the gorge with him! I grab hold of a metal bar that sticks up from the concrete. My arms feel as though they're being torn from my shoulders, but I don't let go. Instead I kick at the fingers with my other foot, the foot that still has a sneaker on it. Those fingers are strong, but they are bone, nothing but bone, and I'm alive, and I am stronger than Skeleton Man. I won't let him defeat me now. I kick again and again and then . . .

The clawed fingers wrapped about my ankle slip free. I hear the one last despairing cry of "Noooooooooo" as Skeleton Man falls away from me like a bad dream disappearing when you wake.

My own hands are slipping. But after all I have been through I can't fail now. I won't let myself fall. I dig in my fingers. My sneakered foot finds a rock for leverage as I push and claw my way up to the top, away from the brink. My heart is pounding like a drum, but I am alive. I breathe in and out as I look at a sky that is filled with the light of the moon and stars. After a while, I inch my way back to the edge and look over. All I can see is darkness and the thin, glittering line of the stream far below, a ribbon of silver touched by the light of the moon. I rub the place where Skeleton Man's fingers scratched my ankle. I can hardly believe it, but I'm perfectly safe at last.

"Molly," a deep voice calls from the main trail below me. "Molly." That voice is worried, almost frantic, but it makes my heart leap with joy.

"I'm here, Dad," I answer. "I'm coming."

Then I go leaping down the trail, my feet as sure as those of a mountain goat. I feel like I can't fall, but even so I stumble just before I reach him.

But he doesn't let me fall. Powerful arms catch me and lift me up, right off the ground, and then my dad is hugging me.

"You saved us, Molly," he whispers into my ear. "You're our Warrior Girl."

"Dad," I sob back. I don't feel like a Warrior Girl at all, just a little kid who wants to cry and cry and cry.

I wish I could say they found my so-called uncle. But they didn't, not on the rocks below or in the swift running stream. Even though the water was high and the current would have carried him down into the deep lake, they should have found him. But they didn't. Where his body went remains a mystery.

So does his real identity. I found my backpack on the trail where I threw it at him, but none of the evidence I gave them and nothing he left in the house gave any clue. They found the doctored photographs, the phony identification papers, all of the stuff in the computer, including the way he was able to hack into banks and databases to get money and information about people. It appeared that he'd chosen our family because of Dad's job with the bank and because he could use me and Mom as leverage to make Dad give him the information he needed. The fact that we didn't have any relatives made it easier for him to deceive people about being my uncle. There was also a diary, with photographs, of how he'd planned everything and carried it out. It was all there, from posing as a highway patrolman to stop their car while they were on their way home that Saturday night to stepping in as my next of kin. Everything was there except who he was and why he did it. And what he was planning to do with us in the end.

"What was it," the school psychiatrist said to me, "that made him want to have total control over a family like that? Was it a chemical imbalance? Perhaps it was because of things that happened to him as a child. Or perhaps not." Then she tapped her pencil against her chin and looked wise. Right.

I remember what my dad and mom said to

me about it all when the police and the reporters and the lights and cameras were finally gone, and there was time at last for us to be alone together.

"There's going to be a lot of people talking about this, trying to figure it all out," Dad said. "But it seems to me that the only place where it makes sense is in our old stories." As he spoke I realized how much the voice of the rabbit in my dreams had been like his voice. "There are still creatures that may look like people but are something else. The reason creatures like Skeleton Man do what they do is that they like to hunt us. The only way to defeat them is to be brave."

He smiled at me then, and I smiled back.

I looked over at my mother and she nodded. But I could tell she had something more to say about it, too, about why he locked them up under the toolshed and barely fed them, why he pretended to be my uncle. Dad and I didn't ask her; we just waited for her to speak.

"Molly," she said, holding my hand tight, "you know what a cat does when it catches a mouse? It doesn't kill it and eat it right away. It plays with it for a while first."

And that was all she had to say about it, though Dad reached over and took both of our hands and we sat there together like that for a long time.

Maybe, like Ms. Shabbas said to me, there never was any real why about it. "Honey," she said, "it happened, but now it is *over*." Then she sang a few lines from that musical about Don Quixote. "Yes, indeed," she said, nodding. "You have dreamed the impossible dream."

I can live with that. Like one of the old stories I've grown up with, something evil came into the lives of good people and we found a way to defeat it. My dad and mom and I are together again, we are happy, and that is enough for me.